D0125643

TYPE: Fire
IMPERIAL HEIGHT: 1'04"
METRIC HEIGHT: 0.4 m

IMPERIAL WEIGHT: 9.5 lbs.
METRIC WEIGHT: 4.3 kg

HOW TO SAY IT: LIT-n

LITTEN

Pokémon™

POPPLIO

TYPE: Water

IMPERIAL HEIGHT: 1'04"
METRIC HEIGHT: 0.4 m

IMPERIAL WEIGHT: 16.5 lbs.
METRIC WEIGHT: 7.5 kg

HOW TO SAY IT: POP-lee-oh

TYPE: Grass-Flying

IMPERIAL HEIGHT: 1'00"
METRIC HEIGHT: 0.3 m

IMPERIAL WEIGHT: 3.3 lbs.
METRIC WEIGHT: 1.5 kg

HOW TO SAY IT: ROW*-let

*Rhymes with NOW

ROWLET

TYPE: Psychic-Steel
IMPERIAL HEIGHT: 11'02"
METRIC HEIGHT: 3.4 m
IMPERIAL WEIGHT: 507.1 lbs.
METRIC WEIGHT: 230.0 kg
HOW TO SAY IT: SOUL-gah-LAY-oh

SOLGALEO

POKÉMON™

LUNALA

TYPE: Psychic-Ghost
IMPERIAL HEIGHT: 13'01"
METRIC HEIGHT: 4.0 m

IMPERIAL WEIGHT: 264.6 lbs.
METRIC WEIGHT: 120.0 kg

HOW TO SAY IT: loo-NAH-luh

POKÉMON

BEWEAR

TYPE: Normal-Fighting
IMPERIAL HEIGHT: 6'11"
METRIC HEIGHT: 2.1 m
IMPERIAL WEIGHT: 297.6 lbs.
METRIC WEIGHT: 135.0 kg
HOW TO SAY IT: beh-WARE

TYPE: Grass
IMPERIAL HEIGHT: 1'00"
METRIC HEIGHT: 0.3 m
IMPERIAL WEIGHT: 7.1 lbs.
METRIC WEIGHT: 3.2 kg
HOW TO SAY IT: BOWN*-sweet

*Rhymes with DOWN

BOUNSWEET

Pokémon

TYPE: Bug-Electric
IMPERIAL HEIGHT: 1'08"
METRIC HEIGHT: 0.5 m
IMPERIAL WEIGHT: 23.1 lbs.
METRIC WEIGHT: 10.5 kg
HOW TO SAY IT: CHAR-juh-bug

CHARJABUG

TYPE: Bug-Fairy

IMPERIAL HEIGHT: 0'04"
METRIC HEIGHT: 0.1 m

IMPERIAL WEIGHT: 0.4 lbs.
METRIC WEIGHT: 0.2 kg

HOW TO SAY IT: KYOO-tee-fly

CUTIEFLY

POKÉMON™

KOMALA

TYPE: Normal
IMPERIAL HEIGHT: 1'04"
METRIC HEIGHT: 0.4 m
IMPERIAL WEIGHT: 43.9 lbs.
METRIC WEIGHT: 19.9 kg
HOW TO SAY IT: koh-MAH-luh

Pokémon™

TYPE: Ghost-Fairy
IMPERIAL HEIGHT: 0'08"
METRIC HEIGHT: 0.2 m

IMPERIAL WEIGHT: 1.5 lbs.
METRIC WEIGHT: 0.7 kg

HOW TO SAY IT: MEE-mee-kyoo

MIMIKYU

POKÉMON™

MUDBRAY

TYPE: Ground
IMPERIAL HEIGHT: 3'03"
METRIC HEIGHT: 1.0 m
IMPERIAL WEIGHT: 242.5 lbs.
METRIC WEIGHT: 110.0 kg
HOW TO SAY IT: MUD-bray

TYPE: Fire-Flying

IMPERIAL HEIGHT: 2'00"
METRIC HEIGHT: 0.6 m

IMPERIAL WEIGHT: 7.5 lbs.
METRIC WEIGHT: 3.4 kg

HOW TO SAY IT: or-ih-KOR-ee-oh

ORICORIO

Pokémon™

PIKIPEK

TYPE: Normal-Flying
IMPERIAL HEIGHT: 1'00"
METRIC HEIGHT: 0.3 m
IMPERIAL WEIGHT: 2.6 lbs.
METRIC WEIGHT: 1.2 kg
HOW TO SAY IT: PICK-kee-peck

TYPE: Water

IMPERIAL HEIGHT: 1'00"
METRIC HEIGHT: 0.3 m

IMPERIAL WEIGHT: 2.6 lbs.
METRIC WEIGHT: 1.2 kg

HOW TO SAY IT:
PYOO-koo-MOO-koo

PYUKUMUKU

Pokémon™

TYPE: Rock
IMPERIAL HEIGHT: 1'08"
METRIC HEIGHT: 0.5 m
IMPERIAL WEIGHT: 20.3 lbs.
METRIC WEIGHT: 9.2 kg
HOW TO SAY IT: ROCK-ruff

ROCKRUFF

TYPE: Electric-Fairy

IMPERIAL HEIGHT: 5'11"
METRIC HEIGHT: 1.8 m

IMPERIAL WEIGHT: 45.2 lbs.
METRIC WEIGHT: 20.5 kg

HOW TO SAY IT: TAH-poo KO-ko

TAPU KOKO

Pokémon

TYPE: Electric-Steel
IMPERIAL HEIGHT: 1'00"
METRIC HEIGHT: 0.3 m

IMPERIAL WEIGHT: 7.3 lbs.
METRIC WEIGHT: 3.3 kg

HOW TO SAY IT:
TOH-geh-deh-MAH-roo

TOGEDEMARU

Pokémon

TYPE: Fire-Dragon

IMPERIAL HEIGHT: 6'07"
METRIC HEIGHT: 2.0 m

IMPERIAL WEIGHT: 467.4 lbs.
METRIC WEIGHT: 212.0 kg

HOW TO SAY IT: TURT-nay-ter

TURTONATOR

Pokémon

VIKAVOLT

TYPE: Bug-Electric

IMPERIAL HEIGHT: 4'11"
METRIC HEIGHT: 1.5 m

IMPERIAL WEIGHT: 99.2 lbs.
METRIC WEIGHT: 45.0 kg

HOW TO SAY IT: VIE-kuh-volt

TYPE: Normal

IMPERIAL HEIGHT: 1'04"
METRIC HEIGHT: 0.4 m

IMPERIAL WEIGHT: 13.2 lbs.
METRIC WEIGHT: 6.0 kg

HOW TO SAY IT: YUNG-goose

YUNGOOS

LUNALA

SOLGALEO